HINNY WINNY BUNCO

CAROL GREENE

PICTURES BY JEANETTE WINTER

HARPER & ROW, PUBLISHERS

Library of Congress Cataloging in Publication Data
Greene, Carol.
    Hinny Winny Bunco.

    Summary: Hinny Winny Bunco, a farmer overworked by
his crabby brother, is miserable until he discovers
his musical talent when he is given a fiddle by a
strange old man.
    [1. Musicians—Fiction.   2. Farm life—Fiction]
I. Winter, Jeanette, ill.   II. Title
PZ7.G82845Hi   [E]   81-47720
ISBN 0-06-022128-3   AACR2
ISBN 0-06-022129-1 (lib. bdg.)

This book is for Carrie

HINNY WINNY BUNCO
AND THE SHABBY OLD MAN

Hinny Winny Bunco lived with his big brother in a house at the edge of the forest. His brother did not like him. He made Hinny Winny Bunco work all the time.

"Hoe the potato patch! Churn the butter! Look for the pig! You arc such a stupid boy, Hinny Winny Bunco!" That's what his big brother said. So Hinny Winny Bunco worked and worked. But he was not happy.

One day a shabby old man came to the house. He wanted a drink of water. Hinny Winny Bunco got it for him. The shabby old man drank. Then he looked at Hinny Winny Bunco. "You do not look happy," he said. "What is the matter?"

"My brother does not like me," said Hinny Winny Bunco. "He makes me work all the time."

"I see," said the shabby old man. "That is not good." He opened his pack and pulled out a fiddle. "Here, take this," he said. "Make music with it, and it will make you happy."

"But I don't know how to make music," said Hinny Winny Bunco.

"You will learn if you really want to," said the shabby old man. "Good-bye." And he walked away into the forest.

Hinny Winny Bunco picked up the fiddle. He tried to make music. *SQUEAK! SQUAWK!* It sounded awful. Hinny Winny Bunco put the fiddle down again.

The next morning Hinny Winny Bunco's brother yelled, "Hinny Winny Bunco! Go hoe the potato patch, you stupid boy!"

Hinny Winny Bunco thought about his fiddle while he was hoeing. Soon he began to hear a song inside his head.

> *Hoe, hoe, rest.*
> *Hoe, hoe, rest.*
> *Turn around.*
> *Stamp your foot.*
> *Hoe, hoe, rest.*

"I like that!" said Hinny Winny Bunco. "I will call it 'The Potato Patch Song.' " He finished his work and ran to play the song on his fiddle.

The next day Hinny Winny Bunco had to churn the butter. While he was churning he heard another song inside his head.

Churna churna THUMP.
Churna churna THUMP.
Churna churna churna churna
THUMP THUMP THUMP!

He learned to play that song on his fiddle too.

Every day Hinny Winny Bunco heard new songs inside his head. He heard "Looking for Pig Song." He heard "Scrub Bucket Song." He heard "Silly Squirrel Song" and "Yelling Brother Song." Soon he could play them all on his fiddle.

Then one day the shabby old man came back to the house. Hinny Winny Bunco ran to get him some water.

"Thank you," said the shabby old man. "Now show me how well you can make music."

Hinny Winny Bunco felt a little scared. He thought the shabby old man looked a little less shabby somehow. What if he thought Hinny Winny Bunco was awful? But Hinny Winny Bunco picked up his fiddle, and listened for a minute to the songs inside his head. Then he began to make music. He played for a long time. Then he stopped.

"That is all," he said. "I don't know any more songs."

"You play very well," said the shabby old man. "And those are beautiful songs. You have worked hard."

Hinny Winny Bunco looked surprised. "But I did not work hard," he said. "I *like* making music."

The shabby old man smiled. "That," he said, "is the best way to work."

HINNY WINNY BUNCO'S SECRET

Hinny Winny Bunco played his fiddle before breakfast. He played it after lunch. He played it between chores. Every night, before he went to sleep, Hinny Winny Bunco tucked that fiddle under his chin and played it again.

"You are having too much fun with that fiddle," said his brother. "You need to do more work. I want you to plant some beans.

"I want beans for supper in just three weeks, or I will take your fiddle away from you."

"That isn't fair," said Hinny Winny Bunco. "It takes beans longer than three weeks to grow."

"That is your problem," said his brother. And off he stomped.

Hinny Winny Bunco planted the beans. Then he thought and thought. At last he had an idea. He picked up his fiddle, tucked it under his chin, and played a special song. It was called "Put Down Your Little Roots and Grow, Grow, Grow Song." He played it every day, and deep in the earth the little beans heard and grew.

Three weeks later Hinny Winny Bunco put a big
bowl of beans in front of his brother.

"How did you do that?" asked his brother. He
looked crabby.

"I worked hard," said Hinny Winny Bunco. "And I have a secret."

"Well, now you must work even harder," said his brother. "I want the cow to give twice as much milk. I want the hens to lay twice as many eggs. And I want the pig to grow twice as fat. All this must happen in three weeks. Or I will take your fiddle away from you."

"That isn't fair," said Hinny Winny Bunco. "The cow and the hens and the pig are doing the best they can."

"That is your problem," said his brother. And off he stomped.

Hinny Winny Bunco took his fiddle out to the barn. He played the cow a special song. It was called "Moo Lullaby Song."

He went to the hen house. He played the hens a song. It was called "Scratch, Scratch, Bugs and Grit Song."

He went to the pigpen and played the pig a song. It was called "Slurping Song."

Every day Hinny Winny Bunco played his special songs for the cow, the hens, and the pig. The songs made them feel warm and good deep inside themselves. And at the end of three weeks the cow gave twice as much milk, the hens laid twice as many eggs, and the pig was twice as fat.

"How did you do that?" asked Hinny Winny Bunco's brother. He looked very crabby.

"I worked hard," said Hinny Winny Bunco. "And I have a secret."

"Well, now you must work even harder," said his brother. "I want you to cut all the hay and put it in stacks by tomorrow. Or I will take your fiddle away from you."

"That isn't fair," said Hinny Winny Bunco. "The hayfield is too big."

"That is your problem," said his brother. And off he stomped.

Hinny Winny Bunco picked up his fiddle and walked to town. He walked right to the middle of the town square. Then he began to play "The Hay-Hopper, Toe-Plopper Song." It was very catchy.

It caught the ears of everyone in town and tickled them. It caught their knees and jiggled them. It caught their toes and wiggled them. Soon nobody in town could stand still. When Hinny Winny Bunco went home to the hayfield, everybody followed him.

They smiled and laughed and danced in the field. They jiggled their knees and wiggled their toes. They cut all the hay and put it in stacks. Then they thanked Hinny Winny Bunco for such a nice time and went home.

"The hay is cut and put in stacks," Hinny Winny Bunco told his brother.

"How did you do that?" asked his brother.

He looked very crabby indeed.

"I worked hard," said Hinny Winny Bunco.

"And now I will tell you my secret. It is my music. But I have another secret to tell you too. I am not going to work for you anymore. You are too crabby. I am going to borrow some money from my friends in town and buy my own farm."

"But who will do all my work?" asked his brother.

"I don't know," said Hinny Winny Bunco. "That is your problem. Good-bye."

HINNY WINNY BUNCO AND MILLIE B.

Hinny Winny Bunco loved his new farm. His crops grew tall and he paid his friends the money he owed them. His animals were happy. Hinny Winny Bunco played special songs for all of them.

Hinny Winny Bunco felt fine. Then one day he saw someone picking flowers. Hinny Winny Bunco thought she was beautiful. He fell in love with her at once. Her name was Millie B.

Hinny Winny Bunco's heart felt as big as a mountain. His knees felt as weak as marshmallows. "I am going to marry that Millie B.," he said, " or my name is not Hinny Winny Bunco."

But first he had to make Millie B. fall in love with him. "Now, how do you make someone fall in love with you?" wondered Hinny Winny Bunco.

"I know! You do something nice for her." So he went to Millie B.'s house and weeded her garden.

It took a long time, and it made Hinny Winny Bunco very dirty. But at last he finished and went to ring the doorbell.

There stood his brother with a big bunch of flowers. "Hello," said Millie B. to his brother. "What pretty flowers! Won't you come in for some tea?"

"Thank you," said his brother. He looked at
Hinny Winny Bunco. "Go away, dirty person," he
said. "Don't bother this lady." Then he shut the
door.

Hinny Winny Bunco went home. "I will not give
up," he said. "I am going to marry that Millie B., or
my name is not Hinny Winny Bunco."

The next day Hinny Winny Bunco baked a big chocolate cake. Then he took a bath, put on his best clothes, and set out to see Millie B.

He was almost there when he heard a splash. "Oh dear!" said Hinny Winny Bunco. He put down his cake and ran to the pond. Right in the middle was a small gray cat. "Don't worry. I'll save you," called Hinny Winny Bunco.

He jumped into the pond and swam out to the cat. But when he got there, the cat said, "Pfft!" and swam to the other side. So Hinny Winny Bunco swam back too.

He shook the water out of his ears and looked around for his cake. It was gone.

"That's all right," said Hinny Winny Bunco. "I will tell Millie B. about the cat instead. It is a funny story."

He went to ring the doorbell. There stood his brother with the chocolate cake.

"Hello," said Millie B. to his brother. "What a lovely cake! Won't you come in for some tea?"

"Thank you," said his brother. He looked at Hinny Winny Bunco. "Go away, wet person," he said. "Don't bother this lady." Then he shut the door.

Hinny Winny Bunco went home. He could not think of any more ways to make Millie B. fall in love with him. This made him feel sad. So he picked up the one thing that always made him feel better—his fiddle. Then he went for a walk.

As he walked, Hinny Winny Bunco played songs about how he was feeling. He played "Heart Like a Mountain Song" and "Knees Like Marshmallows Song." He played "My Brother Took the Cake Song." And then he played "I Love That Millie B. So Much Song." Hinny Winny Bunco played that last song best of all because he meant it deep inside.

"Well, for goodness' sake, why didn't you say so before?" Hinny Winny Bunco could not believe his eyes. There stood Millie B. He had walked all the way to her house.

Hinny Winny Bunco did not know what to say. "Well, never mind," said Millie B. "I love you too. When are we going to get married?"

"Tomorrow!" said Hinny Winny Bunco. And they did.

MILLIE B. SAVES THE DAY

Hinny Winny Bunco and Millie B. lived on the farm for years and years. They were happy. They worked hard, and they had fifteen children.

Hinny Winny Bunco taught his fifteen children to make music too. He taught them to play fiddles and horns, trumpets and flutes. He even taught Melvin, the baby, to play the big bass drum. But most important, he taught them all to play the songs they heard inside their heads.

Soon the whole house was full of music. Everybody played something—everybody except Millie B. She listened.

"Your mother is a good listener," Hinny Winny Bunco told his children. "She is the best listener I know."

"Yes, I am a good listener," said Millie B. "And I like the songs you play. But why don't you make music together sometimes? You could have an orchestra in the parlor."

"That's a good idea!" said Hinny Winny Bunco. "Everybody come to the parlor." Everybody did, and all together they started making music.

BLARE! SQUEAK! TWEEDLE! BLAT! It sounded terrible!

"Stop!" yelled Millie B. "I can't stand it!" She grabbed a pillow and put it over her head.

"I think something is wrong," said Hinny Winny Bunco.

Millie B. took the pillow off her head. "Something *is* wrong," she said. "And I know what it is. You are all playing different songs at the same time. You must all play the *same* song."

"Oh," said Hinny Winny Bunco.

"Oh," said the fifteen children.

Millie B. stood up. "All of you play 'Cat Chasing Tail Song,'" she said. "I will stand here in front of you and wave my arms so you will know how fast to play."

She waved her arms, and everybody played "Cat Chasing Tail Song." They sounded wonderful.

After the song, Hinny Winny Bunco ran over and hugged Millie B. "You really are the best listener I know," he said. "And you are the best wife too."

Millie B. hugged him back. "You are a pretty good husband yourself," she said. "Now let's make some more music."

HINNY WINNY BUNCO VISITS THE KING

More years went by. Hinny Winny Bunco got tired
of being a farmer. He wanted to make music all the
time. But he didn't know how to find a job like that.

One morning he looked at his breakfast and made
a face. "Bah!" he said. "I feel grumpy today."

"Do you?" asked Millie B. "What is the matter?"

"I am tired," said Hinny Winny Bunco. "Besides, I am catching a cold."

"Poor Hinny Winny Bunco!" said Millie B. "You just want to make music all the time. But don't worry. Everything will be all right."

"Bah!" said Hinny Winny Bunco. Then he picked up the newspaper and his mouth fell open. "Look, Millie B.!" he cried. "It says here that the king is sick. He has to stay in bed all day, and nothing makes him feel better."

"How awful!" said Millie B. "Poor king."

"Well, I know what I must do," said Hinny Winny Bunco. "I must go make some music for him. *That* will make him feel better."

So he packed up his fiddle and set off for the palace. Millie B. waved good-bye. "Don't worry!" she called. "Everything will be all right."

But when Hinny Winny Bunco got to the palace gate, the guard would not let him in. "Go away," he said. "The king is too sick to see you."

"I want to make him feel better," said Hinny Winny Bunco. But the guard just shut the gate—tight.

"Drat," thought Hinny Winny Bunco. "Now I must figure out another way to get in. That king needs me."

Just then he saw a cart pull up to the gate. It was full of straw for the king's horses. "Aha!" said Hinny Winny Bunco. He jumped into the cart and hid in the straw. The cart went through the gate, and so did Hinny Winny Bunco.

All that straw made him sneeze, and his cold felt much worse. But he didn't care. He was inside!

Hinny Winny Bunco sneezed all the way to the Royal Bedroom. Then he met another guard.

"Go away," said the guard. "The king is too sick to see you."

"I am going to make him feel better with my music," said Hinny Winny Bunco.

"Don't be silly," said the guard.

Now that made Hinny Winny Bunco angry. He wanted to tell the guard that his music was not silly.

But instead he sneezed a great, huge sneeze.

That sneeze was so huge that it blew the guard down the hall and out the window—into the birdbath below.

Hinny Winny Bunco smiled. Then he blew his nose and went into the Royal Bedroom.

In the middle of the room stood a big bed with curtains all around it. Someone behind the curtains was groaning. "Poor king," thought Hinny Winny Bunco. "I won't even say hello. I'll just make him some music."

He tucked his fiddle under his chin and began to play. He played "Straw in My Ears Song." The groans stopped.

He played "Sneeze the Guard Out the Window Song." Somebody chuckled.

He played "Hurrah for the King Song."

"Whee!" said a voice from behind the curtains. "I think I have died and gone to heaven. Or else that is Hinny Winny Bunco!"

Hinny Winny Bunco knew that voice. But before he could guess whose it was, the curtains opened and out popped—the shabby old man! But he wasn't at all shabby now. He wore a purple nightshirt and a golden crown.

"It's you!" said Hinny Winny Bunco.

"It's me!" said the king. "I always liked you, Hinny Winny Bunco. But now I like you even more. You have made me well again."

"That's all right," said Hinny Winny Bunco. "I like you too."

"Well, then," said the king, "I think you should come and live here in the palace, so you can make music for me all the time."

"Can Millie B. come too?" asked Hinny Winny Bunco. "And my fifteen children?"

"Of course," said the king. "Bring them all. Now play me another song."

Hinny Winny Bunco thought for a minute. He remembered what Millie B. had said. Then deep inside him he heard a song. It was the best song he had ever heard. It was called "Everything *Is* All Right Song." And Hinny Winny Bunco played it for the king.